I LOVE BEING ME!

Written and Illustrated by:

Markita Staples-Green

I love my curly hair.

It keeps all the pretty bows in place!

I love my hands.

They can make such beautiful art!

I love my voice.

Sometimes I talk real loud so mommy and daddy hear me!

I
love
my
brown
skin.

Look at how it glows!

I love my nose.

When I
pinch it
my voice
sounds
funny!

I love my laugh.

When Grandma tells me to relax, it makes me laugh even more!

I love my eyes.

Sometimes I get treats when I open them big and

bright and say

"please"!

I love my lips.

Auntie leaves her lipstick out just for me! Muah!

I love my legs.

Daddy thinks he can catch me but I'm too fast!

I
love
my
tummy.

It's super ticklish!
Hahahahaha!

I love my feet.

Uncle loves when I put them right in his face!

I love my arms.

They fit perfectly around my family.

I love

being me!

My family

loves me too!

Fun little discussion questions:

- What color is your hair?

- What do you like most about your skin?

- What color are your eyes?

- Can you make a happy face?

- Can you make a silly face?

- Are you ticklish?

- Who is in your family?

- What is your favorite part of your body?

- Repeat this phrase:

"I love being me!" "I love being me!" "I love being me!"

THE CURLY CREW

Emmy Miles Cameron Melody Gavin Summer

Thank you for reading!

Have you read the other books in the series? Get them on Amazon and the Curly Crew website!

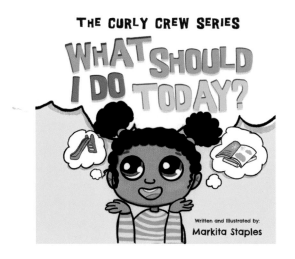

Website & E-mail list: www.curlycrewbooks.com

 @curlycrewbooks

 Curly Crew Books

ⓟ @curlycrewbooks

Made in the USA
Middletown, DE
03 December 2021